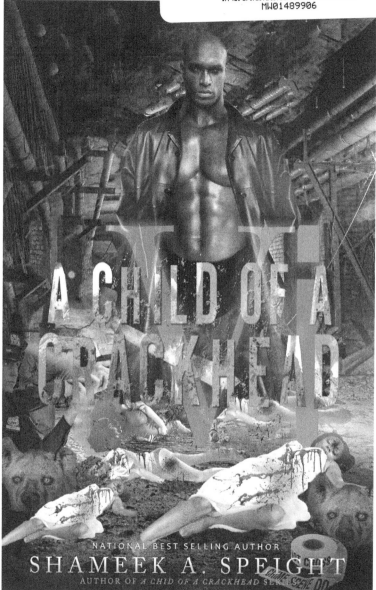

A CHILD OF A
CRACKHEAD

NATIONAL BEST SELLING AUTHOR
SHAMEEK A. SPEIGHT
AUTHOR OF *A CHID OF A CRACKHEAD SER...*

CHILD OF A CRACKHEAD 6.

SHAMEEK SPEIGHT.

ACKNOWLEDGMENTS

I want to say thank you to all the people that have supported my books all these years, and to my new readers, welcome to my sick mind; I hope you have fun. Lol, but if you're looking for an everyday type of story full of love and romance with happy endings, you won't get that here.

My goal is to live up to my name, the king of urban horror, to be one of the greatest storytellers and writers that ever lived, to draw you into a story that you can see in your mind, to have you shocked and say "Oh shit!" but want to keep reading more. My books and stories are one of a kind and will take you to a place you've never been before. There's only one Shameek. A. Speight, one king of urban horror. I created my lane and will do my best to take it to another level. You're about to enter my world, and I hope you enjoy it.

Please leave reviews on Amazon, and feel free to reach out to me and share your experience of reading one of my novels. Your support is greatly appreciated. God bless. I hope you enjoy this book if you're new to my work. To learn more about certain characters like Michael, read A Child of a crackhead series 1-6; to learn about Faith, read Daughter of Black ice 1-5. To learn about Zaira read, I couldn't hear her scream 1-3. All my novels are connected.

Thank you for the love and support.

TABLE OF CONTENTS

SYNOPSIS 1

CHAPTER 1 2

CHAPTER 2 20

CHAPTER 3 31

CHAPTER 4 55

CHAPTER 5 66

CHAPTER 6 81

CHAPTER 7 109

CHAPTER 8 119

A CHILD OF A CRACK HEAD 7. 122

SYNOPSIS

Laughter from the hyenas, echoed throughout the dark woods, as Erica and Carrie ran for their lives, with Adrianna fast behind them and could hear the hyenas eating her friend Donna.

They looked back and could see Black ice and his youngest daughter Zaira standing in the shadows, smiling at them as if this was a game.

Erica slows down as she runs out of breath. All three women stopped and hugged each other and cry hysterically as they realized the stories are real.

Black ice is real and this was their last day on earth.

CHAPTER 1

Each stroke was deeper and felt better than the last one. Rasheed moaned in pleasure as Black ice choked her and looked her in the eyes as he thrust in and out of her with her left leg up.

Why does it feel this good? Why does it feel as if his dick is growing inside me Rasheed thought to herself as she tried to hide how much she was enjoying it, she looked at his sexy chocolate body, the color of rich dark chocolate, every inch of him was pure muscle as if all he did was workout.

Sweat dripped down his forehead and down his chest, with a sexy yet gangster killer look in his eyes as if he would kill you or fuck the shit out of you, you never knew which one, he barely spoke but when he did his voice seemed to travel through your body and touch your soul.

Why is he fucking me like this? Rasheed thought to herself as he turned her around and put her ass in the air and started to give her long deep slow strokes while whining his hips, every time he pushed in her he would grind his hip in a circle motion, making his thick dick tap the walls of her vagina.

"Shh! Yes! Yes baby!" Rasheed moaned as he put one leg up to get deeper inside her then bent over and put his thumb in her mouth.

"Suck it! Suck it bitch!" Black ice said.

Rasheed started to suck his thumb as if it was his penis. The better she sucked it, the better his thrust and stroke was as he smacked her ass.

"Say you like when I slut you the fuck out bitch!" Black ice groaned.

"I love when you slut me out!" Rasheed screamed meaning every word as he started to pound harder and faster.

"Oh my God this is your pussy! This is your pussy!" Rasheed screamed then started biting the black

3

satin sheets as he pounded away harder and faster.

"*Oh God,*" Rasheed screamed and started inching away, so he couldn't beat her pussy up and take some of his penis out.

"*Stop fucking running! Take this dick!*" Black ice demanded and started giving her deep strokes while whining his hips, she tried to crawl away again.

Black ice started to thrust faster then pulled out and put his dick on her face as he exploded, shooting cum on her face.

Rasheed grabbed his dick and sucked the tip of it, he snatched it away and smacked her in the face with his dick four times then walked away.

He just fucked the shit out of me literally. No one dick me down like that in my life. Why did it feel so good? Why did he fuck me like a slut and why the hell did I love it? Rasheed thought to herself as her mind raced and two henchmen entered the bedroom.

She looked at them then Black ice with a confused look.

"Wait, what is going on? I did what you told me. You said I wouldn't have to go back to that dry room with those other women," Rasheed said.

"You won't but I wasn't impressed with you. So, I'll let my daughters have fun with you," Black ice said as he rolled up a blunt.

"What do you mean? What the fuck do you mean let your daughters have fun with me. I'm not a toy!" Rasheed shouted then a henchmen punched her in the mouth and yanked her toward the door and out the room.

She was pulled out the down hallway onto the elevator and rode it down to the third floor.

"Where are you taking me? Please I have no clothes on. May I have something to wear," Rasheed said as she fought the urge to cry and thought how she ended up here.

She closed her eyes and could see herself getting off the train station and someone grabbing her and throwing her into the back of a van. The henchmen went to a double steel door, they opened it and pushed Rasheed in and threw her a white t-shirt and black spandex.

Rasheed watched the double door close and looked around. She could see the night sky full of bright stars and a full moon.

"There is no way I can be outside, I rode down the elevator not up. What is this place?" Rasheed said to herself as she got dressed, then she could hear crying and talking.

"Why does this look like the woods, I'm not going in there, something just don't sitting right with me with this place," Rasheed said to herself then turned around and went back to the steel door and started banging on it.

"Let me back in, I don't want to be in this place! Tell him I'm sorry, I'll do better, I'll take it better! Get me out of here now! Please let me out!" Rasheed shouted then a slot opened in the middle of the door and a long black electric taser, that looked like a night stick came

through the slot and pressed against Rasheed chest and shocked her so hard she flew back into the ground.

"Don't touch the door and if you were smart, you'll run before Zaira and Yana finds you, especially Yana," The henchmen said then closed the slot.

"Zaira and Yana? Who the fuck is that," Rasheed said rubbing her chest.

"Haha! Haha!" Laughter coming from different direction could be heard.

Rasheed looked around as she stood up and could see red eyes staring at her from the dark in the woods, then she turned right and could see more eyes, blinking while looking at her.

Rasheed banged on the double steel door again and the slot opened, she jumped back.

"There is something in here with me, let me out please," Rasheed shouted then could see Black ice looking through the slot.

He blew out thick white smoke through it then inhaled deeply as he pulled on his blunt filled with weed and crack.

"Run bitch! Or I'm going chop your head off and play soccer with it," Black ice said in a deep dark tone.

Rasheed backpedaled knowing he wasn't lying and wouldn't hesitate one second, everything about him screamed killer and not the one to test or play with.

"Fuck you! Fucking asshole!" Rasheed shouted and took off running while looking around. She picked up a thick stick off the ground.

"The moon and stars lit up the night. How am I outside. This makes no fucking sense," Rasheed said to herself then could hear the women talking and crying, she followed the sound until she saw three women dressed in dirty white t-shirts and black spandex with no shoes on.

Rasheed could tell right away they were around her age, late thirties or early forties, one was white.

"Hello! Does anyone know where we at?" Rasheed said and caused the women to jump.

"You scared the living shit out of me girl, don't be sneaking up on people out here after all the shit we been through. You can't just do that," A brown skin woman said the skin tone of peanut butter.

"Anyways, I'm Monica and the white lacy that keep crying!" Monica said, saying crying extra loud.

"That is Betty and that is Staci," Monica said.

"I'm Rasheed do any of you know where we are?" Rasheed said.

"Naw, I was kidnapped by a tall dark-skinned man sprayed something sweet in my face and I passed the hell out. Woke up to a guy putting a pill in my mouth and I can't tell you how high I

was and for how long," Staci replied while fixing her glasses.

"I don't belong here, I'm not supposed to be here, I live in a good suburban neighborhood in Florida, upperclass. I'm a stay-at-home mom, my husband has money," Betty said.

"Uhm, it looks like you stuck in this place with the rest of us Betty, I told you that and there is no point in crying that is not going to fix shit," Monica said.

"You don't understand! They did things to me, three of them made me swallow a pill then my head was spinning and they raped me at the same time. Treated me like nothing, like I was a low life hoe. It went on for hours maybe days I lost track of time I don't know if I been here a few days or a few months. Everyday, was the same thing, forced to take pills and raped. Now I want the pills. I need them. My body is shaking and I miss them. They kept me from thinking and feeling, I'm not supposed to be here," Betty said while crying.

The woman heard a noise and the bush started moving.

Rasheed and the other women turned toward it ready to fight to only see a short stubby woman walk out.

"Uhm, I'm Stephanie younger, I have been hiding in the bushes the whole time listening, trying to see if I can trust you, someone sprayed something on my face and I woke up here and something kept following me, sounds like dogs but then I heard laughter so I hid and heard you all," Stephanie said.

"I would say nice to meet you, but under the circumstance it is not." Rasheed replied.

"So, do anyone know where we are?" Monica asked.

"We're in hell!" Betty said while sitting in the ground rocking back and forth and scratching her arm.

"She's not too far off. I don't know if any of you ever heard the story of Black ice." Rasheed said.

"Yeah, I remember those stories about kidnapped women, they put them in white or black vans, most of the women you never see again, but in some cases, he would release some of the women they'll either be hooked on crack or pregnant by him and his men," Monica said.

"Oh yeah, I remember those stories they were big back in the day. I'm from Detroit and a white van was seen taking women for like two years then it just stopped." Staci replied.

"Well, they are not stories," Rasheed said.

"Psst this sounds stupid! You all sound dumb!" Stephanie stated.

"Why?" Monica replied with an attitude.

"Because you all are talking about stories, those were just stories nothing more about some black guy named Black ice in a leather trench coat. That shit is not real. What's happening to us now is, some type of sex trafficking ring and I'm pretty sure it's not run by any black man or a guy name

Black ice. Just the thought of it kills my brain cells," Stephanie said and rolled her eyes.

"For a person that was kidnapped you sure you know everything, but you're in here stuck like us. Maybe you should listen to what Rasheed have to say. We might learn something. My mother taught me you can learn from a bum on the street or the janitor sweeping the floor. You can learn from anyone if you listen," Monica said.

"Yeah, I'm learning not to be stupid." Stephanie replied.

"Damn you got a bad attitude and know it all huh," Staci said.

"It seems I know more than you all; telling children stories asses." Stephanie replied.

"Listen we're not your enemy, but you're going make it that way. Black ice is real, I know I have seen him, I felt him. He's a real person. Scary as fuck as if he eats souls," Rasheed said.

Stephanie started laughing.

"I'm ready to punch this bitch," Staci said.

"What is so funny?" Monica asked.

"You all! We're in a real-life situation and all of you are talking about an imaginary killer. Fuck Black ice!" Stephanie said.

"Fuck me huh!" The women heard a deep voice say.

They turned behind them to see Black ice standing in the dark with his long leather trench coat on. A machete in his left hand, and an Ed blunt lord in his right.

"Yeah, fuck you! You can't be serious. Get me the hell out of this place. Whatever it is, nigga I'm going to press charges," Stephanie said as she stomped her feet walking toward him, ready to fight, then stopped when she noticed the tallest great Dane dog, she had ever seen in her life step out the brushes and stood next to Black ice.

The side of his face was burnt. He licked his lips and stared at Stephanie as if she was a T-bone steak.

Stephanie nervously stepped back as more dogs came out the bushes but they weren't dogs. Their eyes were red, they weren't as tall as the great Dane dog but weighed as much or more.

They started laughing. Stephanie heart started to race.

"What were you saying? Oh yeah, something about fuck Black ice bitch. See no one fucks Black ice, I do the fucking," Black ice said and pulled in his blunt then patted the great Dane dog on the head.

"This here is Brock, he's very special. I found him in Los Angeles and fell in love instantly. Because you've got such a smart-ass mouth Stephanie younger, you now belong to Brock bitch until he's done playing with you then I'll let my youngest daughter play with you next.

Your rude mouth has gotten your ass into something you won't be able to handle," Black ice said and smiled his devilish grin.

"Brock, get her boy, she's all yours! Go play!" Black ice said while exhaling smoke then snapped his fingers and the hyenas took off running.

"Oh shit! Run!" Rasheed screamed and the other women followed her deeper into the woods as they ran for their lives.

They looked back and could see Stephanie trying to catch up.

"Wait! Wait for me!" Stephanie screamed then felt as if the weight of the world pushed her down.

She could feel large paws on her back. She tried to get up but Brock pushed her back down as if she was a child.

"Wait! Help me! Help me!" Stephanie screamed as the hyenas ran past her and Brock, and she could see the women disappearing into the woods.

"Ahhh!" Stephanie started to scream louder as Brock bit her lightly, ripping her shirt off and

shaking it like a pit bull then bit her thigh as he tore the spandex off.

"He's going to eat me! Help me!" Stephanie screamed as she tried to crawl away and could smell weed mixed with crack.

She could see Black ice sitting on a huge rock, a few feet in front of her smoking.

"Help! I'm sorry! I'm sorry for the disrespect! Don't let him eat me please!" Stephanie cried out.

"Ha ha ha ha!" Black ice laughed his evil laugh and smiled showing off his white teeth.

"Bitch you're going wish he ate you, but I'm sorry Brock is not really into eating people. He does it when hungry but it's not really his thing. I still feed him steaks and shit. You are about to see what his thing is Stephanie younger! I hope you enjoy." Black ice said and smiled as Stephanie tried to figure out what he was talking about.

Stephanie tried to crawl away and Brock grabbed her by the ankle with his teeth and dragged her back. She turned around to fight him. He bit her arm and shook it, then forced her onto her stomach.

"Ahhh!" Stephanie screamed as he sunk his teeth into her left shoulder and was using it to control her, making her move left then right and forced her to arch her back.

What the hell is that? What is happening? Stephanie thought to herself as she felt something that felt like a penis poking her butt looking for her hole, then her heart raced even faster as she realized what was about to take place.

"No! No, get off me! Get the hell off of me!" She screamed but Brock bit down harder, blood seeped out of her shoulders as he slid inside her and started humping fast.

"Ah! Ah!" Stephanie screamed in excruciating pain, not believing what was happening to her.

She tried to move but couldn't, Brock had complete control of her.

Black ice stood up.

"See where your smart-ass mouth got you! More than your ass can handle literally," Black ice said and laughed as he walked off into the woods, twirling his machete.

"Stupid bitch!" He said while pulling on his blunt and exhaling the thick smoke into the air.

"Ahh! Ahh! Ahh!" Stephanie screamed at the top of her lungs, knowing no one was coming to save her.

CHAPTER 2

Rasheed could hear Stephanie screams echo through the woods as she called out for help.

Rasheed looked back and could see the hyenas gaining on them.

"Ahh!" Staci screamed as two hyenas knocked her to the ground and she tried to get up but seven more swarm her.

One bit into the back of her thigh tearing away her flesh. The next one locked its teeth into her side. Her rib bone cracked as it ripped a chunk of her side away.

"Help me! Ah! Help me please!" Staci cried as they rolled her over into her stomach and started laughing.

Three of them mouths and fur was covered in her blood.

"We have help her!" Monica said as they stopped running and watch.

"How? What are we supposed to do? Do you see the sizes of those things, they can push us to the ground easily they are close to the size of a small bear and look how many they are, I counted twenty; let's be realistic while they eating her, it gives us more time to run. How long do you think it's going take them to realize they're all not going to be able to eat her and come after us for a meal.

No, we need to keep fucking moving. I don't want to die like that." Rasheed said.

"You think she does? Look at her!" Monica replied.

"I'm sorry, I have to keep moving," Rasheed said and started walking off.

"Damn she's right! If I stay, I'm dead and if I go help, they will kill me, I can't help no one unless I help myself first," Monica said.

"Please wait! Don't leave me! Help me, Monica!" Staci said weakly then a hyena laughed and ripped open her stomach and started pulling out her intestines and guts.

The hyenas started laughing as they ripped more of her stomach out. Staci cried and wished for death as they ate her alive. Monica took off running after Rasheed. They ran through the woods until their feet hurt.

"I can't go anymore," Monica said.

"We have to keep going or we'll die," Rasheed said as she started power walking then came right to the edge of the woods and looked down and could see a small town.

"Oh shit! We are safe, that is a town! Help! Someone, help us!" Monica said and Rasheed covered her mouth.

"Shh! Are you crazy? You are going to lead those hyenas straight to us and this place isn't what it seems, it looks like we're outside but we're not. I was up when they brought me in here. There's an elevator and we didn't ride it up, it rode down to the third floor. We're underground and somehow, so is this place. Don't be fooled by anything. Let's keep moving, Black ice is still out there somewhere and his men kept talking about his daughters. I don't want to run into them. Can you imagine a child that came from him, I don't even want to picture it, let's go!" Rasheed said as they could hear laughter and Stephanie still screaming deep in the woods.

Rasheed slid down the hill that led into the town, Monica followed closely behind as they looked at the town. There was a street full of store fronts and a big target store.

"Let's go to the Target," Rasheed said as they ran toward it.

They looked behind themselves to see Black ice standing at the top of the hill with seven hyenas standing by his side, looking down at the town and then, he lit up his Newport cigarette filled with crack and smiled, then blew a kiss at Rasheed.

"Eat!" Black ice said and the hyenas started *laughing and took off sliding down the hill.*

"This has to be hell! I have to be in fucking hell! There is no way. I'm thirsty, my feet hurts, I've done step on something harder than my son's Lego and this motherfucker still got hyenas coming after us. I can't get a break," Monica said as they ran into the Target stores.

 The light was dim as they ran through the alleys. Monica stopped at the food alley and grabbed a two-liter Pepsi. She opened it and started drinking it.

"Why didn't you grab water," Rasheed said grabbing a bottle of water and drinking it.

"Fuck that if I'm going die, I'm going drink this damn Pepsi I need sugar, picture me spending my last day on earth drinking water and trying to be healthy, I'm good," Monica said then heard the automatic doors to the store open.

"They are here, we got to keep it moving and find somewhere to hide," Rasheed said.

The sound of hyenas running across the hard floor of the store could be heard as Rasheed and Monica bent low, creeping through the alleyways.

"I feel like I'm going pee on myself," Monica whispered.

"Nobody, told your ass to drink all that soda at a time like this. Just hold it I think I have found a way out of here," Rasheed said as they crept down the shoes ally.

Hyenas laughter could be heard.

"Why do they laugh?" Monica asked.

"I don't know but I think they're talking to each other through the laughter. Shit is weird, I just don't want to get eaten alive like Staci. It looks like she felt every bite and they refused to kill her, it was as if they enjoyed eating her alive and her screams made them happy. I don't want to go out like that," Rasheed whispered as they crept to the back foot of Target.

"Pshh! Pshh! This way!" Rasheed and Monica could see a woman dressed like them in the back of the store storage area, waving at them to come.

Monica and Rasheed ran toward her and hid in an alleyway.

"I'm Erica, I can help you, we have to get out of this store, Zaira hunts in here all the time, it's the first place people run to all the time, I tried to save as many as I can but it's hard," Erica said.

"Who is this Zaira?" Monica asked.

"One of Black ice's daughter, you don't want her to get her hand on you, her knives leave you

paralyzed and she does inhumane things to you after but now is not the time. Those hyenas are in a hurry and can smell you all, we got to keep it moving," Erica said as she picked up a brown book bag she had filled up with supplies.

"What is this place?" Monica asked.

"Girl be quiet. Let's just follow her," Rasheed said as they followed Erica to a back door, then Rasheed made a funny gasping sound.

Monica turned around to see Black ice standing directly behind Rasheed and his machete pushed through her back and poked out of her stomach.

"I just had to get inside you one last time." Rasheed heard Black ice whisper in her ear, his lips touching her earlobe as her body shook, and blood dripped out of her mouth. She coughed up blood.

"The funny thing is you ran from the dick but you are taking this a whole lot better, if you were this tough the first time you wouldn't be here," Black

ice said then twisted the machete blade in a circle while it was still inside her.

He yanked it out and swung in one swift move. Rasheed looked at Erica and Monica while crying, with blood dripping out the corner of her mouth.

"Ah!" Monica screamed at the top of her lungs as Rasheed body dropped to the ground hard and her head sat on the machete blade while it was jammed into the wall on the left side of them.

Rasheed blinked her eyes and tried to talk not knowing her head was no longer attached to her body. Her body thumped around on the ground like a chicken when you chop its head off.

Black ice smirked showing Erica and Monica his devilish grin as he grabbed Rasheed's head off his machete that was still jammed on the wall.

 He placed the head on the ground and started kicking it around like a soccer ball. He kicked it left, then right, he kicked it up and bounced it on his knees then kicked it to Monica who caught it in her hand as a reflex.

"Ah! Ahh!" Monica hollered as she held Rasheed's detached head and her eyes were still opened, and moving around.

Urine ran down Monica's leg, as her body trembled in fear.

"See, I have theory that the head is still alive for a while until the brain realizes it's not getting any oxygen or blood. So, after I chop a person's head off, they still see and feel things, just look at her facial expression. She's still alive in there," Black ice said then laughed.

"But seriously kick it back, I wasn't done playing, she got a big ole head," Black ice said in a deep demanding tone.

"Ah!" Monica screamed once more and dropped Rasheed's head and took off running after Erica who was already outside and down the block running for her dear life.

"She's a screamer I think I want her," Yana said as she stood next to her father Black ice.

She was dark-skinned in complexion like him and just turned twenty.

"You and Zaira can have the rest; I just wanted this one, she pissed me off, but kick the head to me princess," Black ice said as Yana walked over to Rasheed's head and kicked it to him and he kicked it back to her and Zaira his youngest daughter came out of hiding and joined the game. They kicked Rasheed head to each other while laughing and smiling and ten hyenas watched patiently waiting for them to be done with their fun so they can devour Rasheed's body.

CHAPTER 3

Stephanie couldn't believe what had happened to her after three hours of Brock doing things she didn't think was possible to her, she laid on her stomach, on the ground, body beaten up and bleeding not moving as Brock circled around, sniffed between her legs and sniffing her butt then licked her face.

"Please no more! Please I can't take anymore." Stephanie cried and whimpered, as her lips trembled in fear.

"This can't be real. It has to be a nightmare. Stuff like this doesn't happen in real life, but the pain is real, God please help me, lord forgive me for my sins. Our father who art in heaven hallowed be his name, his kingdom come, his will be done on earth as if in heaven, give us this day our daily bread and forgive us of our debts as we forgive debtors, and lead us not into temptation but deliver us from all evil, for thy is the kingdom, the power and glory forever in Jesus name we pray amen. God help me, please make this a terrible nightmare, let me wake up in my bed covered in sweat and my mind forget this dream in seconds," Stephanie said.

"Hmm, I'm sorry to tell you lady this isn't a dream or a nightmare and God is not going to deliver you from the hands of the evil one, matter of fact

that is exactly the hands you are going to," Yana said.

Stephanie looked up to see a young dark-skinned girl in a black body suit, smiling down at her. Brock walked over to her and she pet him on the head as if he was a normal dog.

"That! That animal you need to get away from it! It's not right! It has done things to me!" Stephanie said and sounded as if she was trying to hold back from crying.

"Who Brock? Yeah, Brock is different, the first time I saw him work, I was in shock, trust me it takes a lot to shock me, but my father said Brock was born like that, just like I was born the way I was. But he's a good dog, I guess to me and my siblings. The family secret is that we can literally talk to animals, get inside their heads and understand them, not just animals, insects too but that is more of Zaira's thing but I can control spiders.

They do whatever we order. There's a lot of benefit to being a child of the Devil. You wouldn't believe me if I told you, like we can heal instantly. Shit is crazy," Yana said.

"Help me please, get that dog away from me," Stephanie said weakly, as Yana put a bottle of water in front of her.

"No, I can't help you, I want to eat you, but then I'll have to fight Zaira and her short little ass is mean, she tried to kill me and my other sisters about four times already," Yana said.

Stephanie opened the bottle and started drinking the water, the more she drank, the better she felt.

"What is in this?" She said then looked at the bottle and drank more.

"I added adrenaline and a little fentanyl into the water. My father manufactures the pills and sells them on a large scale and feeds them to the people we kidnapped. The adrenaline I added to the water is to get you hyped up, I want to see how long you'll last with Zaira, oh I'm talking to you because I miss my other sisters, I really don't

like Faith or Zaira both of them tried to kill me repeatedly, not a good way to bond with your sisters right.

But I'm a triplet and I miss my real sisters. Ayana who I can't find, somewhere being crazy and scary Macy my other sister who is out in the world probably eating people, she has a thing for eating whole families.

Zaira and Faith don't like us because we're cannibals but like Brock we were born that way, but if they just try a little piece of human flesh they would understand," Yana said while smiling and picturing eating Stephanie.

"You all are crazy! The whole fucking family!" Stephanie said as she was shocked that she could stand up, she couldn't feel the bite on her legs and shoulders as bad, but her vagina and anal was sore and throbbing still.

She looked at Brock standing next to Yana and started crying. Yana threw one black t-shirt to her and she caught it, she quickly put it on. It came down to her knees.

"Why are you helping me?" Stephanie asked.

"I see there's no point talking to you, I told you I'm not helping you, if it was up to me, I'll cut your liver out and eat it raw. But you pissed off my father with your mouth, so he gave you to Brock and normally lets Brock keep his play things until he kills them, but again you had a smart-ass mouth so my father giving you to Zaira, I want to piss Zaira off, she doesn't like to chase people.

So, drink more of that water, don't let her knife touch your skin. The moment it does, it's over for you. Now run about a mile in that direction there is a town and places for you to hide," Yana said.

"What about Brock and the hyenas?" Stephanie said not trusting her.

"Stupid I told you we control the animals. You dying fast isn't in the plan so run, Zaira is coming," Yana said.

Stephanie finished the water and took off running as fast as she could through the woods.

Zaira jumped out of a tree and looked at Yana up and down.

"You're a real bitch for that!" Zaira said in sign language.

"Don't get mad at me because you are short with little legs, go get her little sister before she finds that Erica bitch, you know how that goes. Once Erica gets them it's hard to find them in this place, I don't think father would like that." Yana said in sign language while smirking.

Zaira pulled out one of her knives and thought about attacking Yana. Yana pulled out a short sword.

"Your other two psychopath aren't here to help you," Zaira said.

"So, you think I still won't kick your ass little sister. Father said we can't kill each other, he never said I couldn't eat one or two of your fingers in pickle juice," Yana said and smirked just thinking about it, but knew beating Zaira would be easier said than done.

She was the youngest of Black ice children but the grimiest and most ruthless one out them all.

"I'm going make you cry again one day like I did when I killed your best friend, Osis bitch!" Zaira said in sign language and took off running.

 "I really can't stand that little girl, why couldn't I have a sweet nice little sister, no I had to have this mean insane little bitch that I don't know if she loves you or wants to kill you." Yana said to herself.

"Come on Brock let's go get something to eat. You are lucky you don't have any siblings it is not what it is made up to be. They really know how to push your buttons and hurt your feelings. That little bitch just hurt my damn feelings. I'm going punch her in the face when I see her again," Yana said as she walked off with Brock by her side.

"I can't believe the energy I have, it's like I ate a ton of fucking sugar or I feel sixteen again jumping rope outside," Stephanie said to herself as she ran as fast as she could and didn't feel tired.

She jumped over a bush, she slowed down and could see hyenas hiding in the woods. Their red eyes growling just looking at her.

"She said they wouldn't mess with me I just got to get to the town," Stephanie said out loud then her vagina started to hurt.

She stopped running and started crying as flashbacks of what Brock had done to her played in her mind. She heard a tree branch break and turned around, she looked all around then looked up.

Four trees down, a little dark-skinned girl with her hair in a ponytail tail sat on a branch of a tree, dressed in all black body suit.

She stared at Stephanie; Stephanie continued to look at her until the girl smiled. Stephanie's heart raced and start beating funny. The smile was the same as Black ice, that devilish grin looking like the cat that swallowed a bird. Pure evil and devious.

"Zaira!" Stephanie said and took off running, she looked back and couldn't believe what she was seeing. Zaira was leaping from tree to tree like a chimpanzee.

"Is this girl a squirrel? What the fuck is up with this sick ass family, there are no normal people in it," Stephanie said as she ran even faster then saw a knife slam into the ground in front of her feet, just missing her.

She stopped and looked at it but moved her head just in time as the knife came out of the ground and flew backward.

Stephanie looked back and watched the knife return to Zaira's hand who was two trees down looking at Stephanie and smiling.

"What the hell!" Stephanie said and started running again.

"This can't be real life and why are they always fucking smiling, just staring and fucking smiling at you all happy and shit. This can't be life. God please let this be a dream I'm running from

someone half my damn size," Stephanie said to herself as her energy started to die down and she slowly started feeling the pain in her body caused by Broke.

"I'm must be running through all the adrenaline Yana gave me, I can't slow down," Stephanie said then looked back and could see Zaira still jumping from tree to trees on all fours.

Stephanie could see the lights coming from the town she ran and tripped over her feet and rolled down the long hill.

"Ouch!" Stephanie said and rubbed her head then lower back.

"I'm way too old for this bullshit," Stephanie said and looked up to see Zaira at the top of the hill smiling then jumped and started sliding down the hill on her feet.

"Psst, this is just too fucking much! I want to cry," Stephanie said, got up and started running.

She noticed a few stores and ran to the subway.

"Help! Help anyone, please help me! A crazy little girl is chasing me and there are dogs and hyenas outside!" Stephanie shouted then noticed the subways had no one in it.

She ran behind the counter then ran back down and out the stores as her mind replayed what Rasheed said.

"The bitch said we're not really outside and this is like a movie set but how can that be, everything looks real and the air is fresh with breeze. This can't be," Stephanie said then saw a restaurant and ran inside of it.

She looked around and it was completely empty. She ran to the back as the restaurant door opened and hide up underneath the table.

"I know you are in here! No one can hide from me! I'm deaf but my gift allows me to hear in other ways. There is no point in trying to run, all it does is make me bored. I don't even like killing your type. You all are civilians to me, my father and sisters like it; I don't know why.

I like killing serial killers, real killers, people like me, now that is fun; I kill you people to impress my father.

Shit is so sad, I'd rather try to kill one of my sisters at least they can give me a good fight," Zaira said as she pulled out a chair from one of the tables and sat down.

"Like I said, I really don't hurt you I rather someone that going put up a better fight, but my father is kind of scary as you can see. You pissed him off and now see what is happening to you. I'll be damned if I make him mad at me," Zaira said then stood up.

She stomped the floor and vibration went out and came back to her and she knew exactly where Stephanie was, her being deaf give her an extra gift, so she could feel people heart beats in her body, she could use sound wave to bounce back to her body like bats and dolphin echolocation.

It allowed her to see through walls and buildings, it was her special gift from being the devil's daughter.

Stephanie noticed Zaira stopped talking. She listened to see if she could hear her footsteps but didn't hear anything. She looked around while underneath the table to see if she could see Zaira legs or feet but she didn't see anything.

Damn, where did that little crazy bitch go, maybe she left. Stephanie thought to herself as she peeled her head out from underneath the table and Zaira grabbed her by her hair.

She tried to pull free but was surprised at how strong she was.

Zaira punched her in the face and pulled her from underneath the table, then let go of her hair.

"There is no way I'm going let some little bitch half my size man handle me. Come little girl I'm going to give you the ass whopping your daddy

and momma should have given you," Stephanie said as she stood up and put her hands up ready to fight.

She swung at Zaira, and Zaira dodged it with ease. Stephanie swung twice and missed.

"Stay fucking still you little cunt!" Stephanie shouted then swung again; this time, Zaira grabbed her wrist and squeezed it.

"Ahh! Ahh!" Stephanie screamed and looked at Zaira as if she was a monster.

Her grip was stronger than any man's grip, Zaira looked at her and smiled her evil devilish grin and twisted her wrist.

A snapping sound echoed through the restaurant as it broke.

"Ahh! Oh God no! Lord no!" Stephanie screamed in excruciating pains as Zaira let her go and smiled at her.

Stephanie held her wrist and took off running.

"What is she? What the fuck is she? There is no way she's that strong. How is it this possible? How is any of this probably. God, please save me from these demons," Stephanie said as she ran to the kitchen.

It was all white with bright lights and steel tables and pots. Stephanie grabbed a chrome knife and started walking backwards as Zaira came through the kitchen door holding a knife.

"Stay back, God protect me!" Stephanie screamed as Zaira threw a knife at her.

The knife sliced Stephanie on the thigh. Stephanie started to feel light headed, and stumbled.

"What the hell is wrong with me. Why do I feel so damn weak, what did you do to me?" Stephanie said weakly as she fell on the floor.

"Don't let my sister's knife touch your skin, the littlest cut will leave you paralyzed."

Yana's words played in Stephanie's mind.

"This is what she meant," Stephanie said to herself as she tried to move but couldn't, then Zaira came and sat down on her chest.

"Just kill me! Kill me and get it over with! I can't keep running for my life. I can't be scared," Stephanie said as she tried to move her legs or hands but couldn't.

"You can stop trying to move, my knives are covered in a special liquid I made to paralyze my victims and make them high," Zaira said as she sliced Stephanie on the arm twice.

"I kind of feel bad for you, because what my father have planned for you is worse than death itself. You're not allowed to die anytime soon, no hyenas will touch, me or my siblings won't touch you. I don't know what you said to make him so angry, but he wants you suffer. Shit, only one thing is worse than me and Brock, that is becoming one of my sister Faith pets.

Now that is fucked up, you wouldn't want that but it's still not worse than what Brock does to people. That's just nasty and disgusting. The thought of it makes me want to vomit and my sisters wonder why I don't like big dogs. I'll take the hyenas and insects anyway," Zaira said as she pulled a few things out from her hostler on her belt.

"What are you going do to me if you are not going kill me?" Stephanie asked nervously.

"I'm going to fuck you up for the rest for your life, make you wish you was dead. This is the fun part for me, I guess you should be happy, I just collect body parts. Yana eats them," Zaira said then twisted her facial expression up in disgust, then picked up her small spoon.

She grinned her devilish smile as she pried open Stephanie's left eye lid.

"Wait! Wait, what are you doing?" Stephanie asked then screamed in agonizing pain as Zaira jammed the spoon into the corner of her eyes and pushed it in.

"It's really science to do this, I got good after my tenth time. The art is not to pop the eyeball but

get it all out in one piece, now I can do it in my sleep. I guess the saying is right, practice makes perfect," Zaira said talking while Stephanie screamed at the top of her lungs, but Zaira couldn't hear because she was deaf.

Every time Stephanie talked, she was reading her lips. She scooped out Stephanie's left eye ball and placed it on a cloth, then she pried open Stephanie's right eye lid.

"Ah! Ahh! No! No! God save me! God help me!" Stephanie cried out while trying her hardest to tell her body to move, to do anything but it wouldn't listen as Zaira jammed the spoon into the corner of her eye, pushed it in and scooped it out.

"I had to learn to get the right sized spoon, I had to make custom spoons, the first one I used back in the day was too big. I perfected my craft.

What's funny is all my siblings have a thing. Mine is that I take my victims eyes and tongues and keep them in jars. My father takes people heads and hands and put them in jars. My brother does heads as well. Faith takes it to another level and just chops off most of your body parts and still keep you alive. I think she's sick in the head. Then you got the triplets, now they're scary and always hungry for some strange reason.

They eat brains and everything else in their victims, I'm not surprised I heard their mother was like that too and is bipolar. My siblings say I talk a lot to be deaf, you think I talk a lot, of course you don't," Zaira said as she turned Stephanie's head and grabbed her knife and started slicing off her left earlobe.

"Ahh! Ahh!" Stephanie screamed while trying to cry but couldn't her eyes were gone, nothing but a black eye socket was left as Zaira sliced off her ears.

Zaira grabbed her by the chin and turned her head right.

"Faith said I'm jealous that people can hear that's why I collect earlobes, I don't think so I'm okay with being deaf my mother taught me it's not a handicap, but a gift and it is. I smell better, my

skin sense things better, everything is better about me.

I wouldn't want it any other way but my sister Faith said I'm suffering from a deep-rooted-issues, whatever that is supposed to mean. She acts like she doesn't keep her mother in a cage with no legs and arms, talking about deep rooted issues.

It's hard being the youngest everyone thinks you're emotionally unstable. I'm really not, I just want my father to look at me how he looks at Faith; like she's the most evil thing in the world," Zaira said as she placed Stephanie's earlobe on the cloth next to the other one then grabbed Stephanie's chin and threw a pill in her mouth forcing her to swallow it.

"Antibiotics, I have to give it to you so you don't get an infection, my tools are clean and all but it still has to be done, you'll get a lot of that from our nurse. Father said he wants to keep you alive for a year because of your smart-ass mouth Stephanie younger, personally I'll try to run into a tree repeatedly if I was you, a year belonging to

Brock; I'll kill myself but he's not going allow that.

He has nurses and doctors down here, he's an evil fucking genius, highly intelligent. I guess that we're me and my siblings got it from," Zaira said as she grabbed her pliers and pried open Stephanie's mouth.

She used the pliers to grab and lock onto her tongue then grabbed her knife and started sawing away until she pulled half of Stephanie's tongue out.

Stephanie started choking on her own blood from her tongue while crying. She felt Zaira grab her tongue again than something burning hot press onto where the open wound was.

"Ughh! Ughh!" Stephanie groaned in pain as she tried to scream and her body trembled.

"Oh look! You'll be able to move soon, I normally don't burn the tongue wound but father said you must stay alive. It's a trick I learnt from my sister Faith. She's great at keeping people alive after

she chops their body parts off," Zaira said put another pill into Stephanie's mouth.

"This will get you high and help with the pain. I don't want you to get a heart attack. The fentanyl pills are crazy strong. So, you'll be okay for a day, well it was nice meeting you. Thank you for your eyes they are beautiful," Zaira said as she picked up the cloth with Stephanie eyeballs, earlobes and tongue in it.

"It's going straight into a clear blue jar," Zaira said as she skipped like a little girl out of the kitchen then restaurant.

"Ahh! Ahgh!" Stephanie cried and made a funny sound because she had no tongue. She tried to move but only could move her finger tips.

"This can't be real," she said with tears in her voice but sounded like a new born speaking.

The fentanyl pill started to kick in, numbing the excruciating pain she was in.

"Hello! Hello, is someone there?" Stephanie said while still crying.

She could hear footsteps approach her. She tried hard to see, not wanted to believe that her eyes were really gone but they were.

Her heart raced as she felt something brush past her leg but couldn't move, then she felt something breathing on her face, then a long tongue licked her face.

Stephanie knew that tongue, she felt it before.

"No! No! Lord No!" She cried in a whiny tone as Brock sunk his teeth into her shoulder and rolled her over onto her stomach.

"No! Not again! Not again!" Stephanie cried but her cries for help went unnoticed and no one was coming save or help her.

CHAPTER 4

―――――― ⌈⌍ ――――――

"Michael!" Rachel said as she jumped up from her sleep and grabbed her shotgun that was by her bed, she scanned her bed then got out of it and opened her room door for anything but didn't see anyone. She then checked her whole three-bedroom house.

"Thank you Jesus for keeping me safe. Keep the devil away from me, and give me peace of mind Lord. Hallelujah," Rachel said then went to her night stand and grabbed holy water on the nightstand and started sprinkling it around every corner of her house.

"Bless my house lord, keep evil away from my house lord, keep those who want to do me harm away, don't let me entertain them. If they enter lord, let them be filled with your spirit and presence O lord. Let them change their ways lord or run from fear, because my God is a mighty God. He can do anything but fail.

Thank you Jesus, thank you for loving me. Thank you for loving my son, thank you for loving my grandbaby. It's not who they come from but how you can use them lord. Use them great things lord, let them touch the world but don't let the world touch them lord," Rachel said then dropped down to her knees.

"I'm nothing without you God, I am weak without you old. Please protect me, protect my son. He's not himself, keep him safe God, I beg you lord, he has lost his way, he lost sight of what matters. God, he needs you to guide him father as you guide me. You took me from being a crackhead to healing me and making me stronger.

I hear you when you speak to me, please hear my prayers. Please protect my son, in Jesus name I pray amen," Rachel said then got up and grabbed her cellphone and called her son.

Michael stood on the edge of a roof to a seven-story building, staring at a warehouse. The breeze blew on his face once in a while from the cool night air. He could feel his phone vibrating in his trench coat pocket.

He pulled it out to see the call I.D read mom and out the phone back in his pocket.

"I know you're there I'll get you bastard I swear," Michael said then heard his mother voice in his ear repeatedly as if she was standing right next to him.

"Michael! Michael!"

Michael turned around and looked for her but knew she wasn't there but he could feel her presence all around him.

"Mother!" He mumbled, then pulled his phone out and answered the call.

"Hey sweetie, it took you long enough. You know I hate when you don't answer right away," Rachel said.

"That is why you did the creepy thing, where I can feel you next to me or hear you in my head." Michael asked, for as long as he has known his mother was different, she had dreams and could see the future, she had a bad feeling and would

tell him and would be ready, then she had a gift of calling him in his head or when he fell asleep.

Michael barely talked about it because it couldn't be explained. It was just something she did after she got off drugs.

"We'll if you would have answered the first call, I wouldn't have to call you the other way, but I didn't call to discuss that. I had a dream baby and know what you're doing, don't do it. Come home to me, let's us pray on it and let me cook for you. You're not in the right state of mind," Rachel said.

"There is nothing to pray about I'm going kill my father for once and all. There will be no coming back for him, he can't continue to keep getting away with hurting people and hurting me," Michael replied.

"No, that is not your job, God will take care of him." Racheal replied.

"When? When will God take care of him cause I'm thirty years old and he has been running the

streets before I was born. Killing people and finding loop holes to stay alive and young. So, when will he take care of him, mom? I'll tell you when. Never.

Nothing bad ever happens to the fucked-up people in life the bad people they get more blessings than the faithful." Michael shouted.

"That is not true baby, they pay for their sins. I need you to come home the path you are walking down will get you killed. I saw your death in my dreams Michael, you can't beat him, not now, you have no one. You think I don't know but I know Mike is dead, I dreamt about his death as well, your sister killed him. I know what is going on baby I can see it." Rachel replied.

"If you can see so much, how come you didn't warn me that my father is going to kill Envy, how come you didn't stop me from killing my son, Evan explain that to me mother," Michael said.

"I didn't see Envy's death you know my gifts don't work like that. I see what God allows me to see, as far as Evan goes baby, you didn't kill him. I had

the dream and saw what you were going do because you aren't yourself, I put the dream in your head to make you think it was real.

Evan is safe and with a friend of mine that is taking care of him," Rachel said.

"You put the dream in my head, what do you mean? I don't understand." Michael replied.

"It's complicated son, but God had shown me what you were going do. You thought of it. So, I was able to put it in your head so you can see it and feel it and think it was real, that's not the first time I have done that to you.

I did it once when you were a child, your son is fine, you can have him back once I know you mind straight and we start praying together again.

You're lost and hurting. I saw all the people you have been killing in my dreams. You can't keep doing that, do you know the deal your ancestors made with the devil.

For the gifts that you all have? If you don't know I'll tell you. For every person you kill, or if anyone with Black ice blood in them kills someone, that person automatically goes to hell even if they were good, their souls go to the devil; that is the curse of your bloodline baby.

All those innocent women your father killed they will go to hell, condemning souls to the devil. I need you to stop and come home," Rachel said.

Michael got quite

"I thought I killed him, I thought I killed my own son mother, I was hurting," Michael said while crying.

"I know baby, your mother knows, but I need you to come home please. You're by yourself, you can't face your father like that, you always had Envy and Mike," Rachel stated.

"I'm not alone I have some men from the catholic church, anointed soldiers." Michael replied and wiped his tears.

"Son you can't trust the catholic church, you're better off with a Muslim or Christian, but not Catholics; they don't like people of color, how many blacks you see that are catholic?

They will cross you. You have no one you can trust baby, listen to your mother I have never lied to you my black gold, my black king. Don't let this world touch you. That is what I always told you?" Rachel said.

"You said I should to touch the world but, I shouldn't let it touch me but mother it did touch me, it killed my wife, my best friend, he did it, just to make me like him," Michael said while crying and holding back his tears.

"We can figure this out, I raised you to be strong, you are your father's son but you are my child first, I love you more than life itself. Now listen to me and bring your butt home. My dreams are never wrong Michael, if you go forward with your plan you will die, your father is bigger and stronger and has more resources and he won't hesitate to harm you, he wanted you to be like him your whole life and the fact you weren't

bothered him but now he has Faith he feels you're replaceable. His oldest daughter is more like him. I saw her in my dreams as well, I see all his children. God shows me, he shows me because we are supposed to fight him together son." Rachel said.

"I'm not listening to more of this bullshit mother, I'm no longer Michael my name is Evil, stay out my head and out my dreams. I'm going kill your daddy I swear!" Michael said then hung up the phone and went back to at looking at the warehouse.

"Michael! Michael, my son I love you. My black gold."

Michael could hear his mother voice in his ears.

"Stop! Stay out my head and dreams I'm doing this no matter what. Leave me alone," Michael said out loud then he couldn't feel his mother presence anymore it was as if she walked away.

When she whispered in his ears it always felt as if she was standing right next to him.

"I know he is in there, he has to be, I can feel his energy," Michael said to himself.

"One of the gifts of being a child of Black ice, they could sense when one of them was near, a dark energy letting them know that someone in their bloodline was close by.

My father has to die after what he did to Envy, he has to pay," Michael said out loud to himself as he started crying.

"I will kill the devil" he mumbled to himself then texted his men to get ready.

Rachel lit a new port cigarette and poured her a cup of Pepsi as she walked back and forth.

"Why don't children listen. The dreams don't lie, if I knew where he was, I'll stop him, I don't care if he's a grown man. He's still my baby, he is surrounded by wolves. If I try to call him and get in his head again, he's just going to push me out. I don't know what to do," Rachel said talking out loud as her left eye started to twitch from being agitated.

She smoked the new port cigarette fast then lit another one. She dropped to her knees.

"Oh lord please, I beg you please for once let my dreams be wrong, let me be the crazy religious lady my son thinks I am," Rachel said as images of her dream flashed in her head of her son fighting Black ice and Black ice stabbing him.

"Lord please protect my baby; I know he is a sinner but please God he is all I have." Rachel prayed all night while rocking back and forth.

CHAPTER 5

"We got to help her!" Monica said.

"There is no helping anyone without helping yourself. You hear her screaming, that means Zaira or Brock have her." Erica replied.

"You said Zaira is nothing but a child a pre-teen surely we can take her out together," Monica said.

"If you haven't noticed nothing is normal with these people, if I tell you half the things they can do. You'll think I'm lying and this is a dream. Just because Zaira is young doesn't mean we can beat her. All Black ice children have martial arts training, they train everyday but now not the time to discuss this. We got to make sure Zaira is gone so we can go," Erica said as she stood close to a house generator.

"Let's move," Erica said then ran down the block, then cut through the backyard.

She walked to a tool shed that was in a backyard, opened the door and went in, Monica followed her. Erica moved a lawnmower to reveal a trap door.

Erica lifted it up and smiled, *"come we can't stay up here for long, something will find us, we got to worry about Black ice, his children and Brock or the hyenas, let's go,"* Erica said and Monica went down the stairs as Erica closed the trap door behind them put the lawnmower over it.

"Please help me understand, I'm so confused and lost," Monica said as she walked faster down the stairs to see there was a tunnel made of dirt.

"What do you want to know, I'll do my best to break it down," Erica said and passed her a flash light.

"Okay start with what the hell this is and why we're not hiding in one of those houses. They are big, and like three blocks of them," Monica said.

"The hyenas will find us, if not then Zaira. Zaira has a gift where vibrations bounce off her, but I

learned the generators next to the home distort that gift, that is what they call it a gift. I learned hiding underneath the ground is safer, so I dug tunnels through all the homes," Erica said as they walked down the tunnel.

"How did you pull that off and how did the hyenas and that big dog, what did you called him. Oh yeah, Brock how come they didn't find you then?" Monica asked.

"Surprisingly there is a lot of food and supplies in this place. This place is Black ice and his children's hunting ground. They use it to have fun and not hunt outside. There is lot of food in here.

I took black pepper and poured it around the house and everywhere I walk. It fucks up the hyenas nose. They can't sniff me out, they start crying and run back into the woods, they live there and they are more than I can count," Erica said and turned right.

Erica told Monica as they came up to a floor in the tunnel.

"How long have you been here to dig this? And why do you help people?" Monica asked.

"I have been here maybe two or three years, I lost track of time," Erica said and held her head down.

"How come they didn't kill you yet?" Monica asked with a confused look on her face.

"I keep escaping, the first time I got away and a lot of my friends were killed. I was free then my sister got kidnapped, I called the F.B.I they didn't want to believe that a black man could run and organize sex traffic ring, my stupid ass didn't have a clue how organized it really was and how deep it went, I learned that anyone could be a henchman, people, F.B. I, nurses.

I was double crossed by a woman I escape with then my sister, I found out she was pregnant with Black ice's child," Erica said.

"That is still not answering the question. Why are you still alive? And if you can escape, can you do it again?" Monica asked.

"No, I can't escape, that is one of the reasons I'm still alive, I'm the only one that have escaped in years; so, he let me live to study how I got away to learn the weaknesses in his system or compound base.

The second reason why I'm still alive they can't catch me. I studied them and I learned.

The third reason is, I think he wants me to be a henchman, no I know he wants me to be one, he likes my survival skills," Erica said.

"So, it's live like this, be hunted or join him, and your sister now happens to be his baby mother, and you choose to still hide and run! Yeah, you're crazy," Monica said.

"You are saying that now because you don't understand what they do and what it takes to be a part of them, they kidnap innocent people sell their organs or sell them as sex slaves overseas.

Then there is the drugs manufacturing and selling and the room with women hooked on the fentanyl pills and crack. All of that still doesn't *compare to what he and his children or that big dog Brock the size of a small damn horse does to people. I have seen what he does to people, I know why that woman was still screaming as we went down here,"* Erica said.

"I don't know, you know all of these yet you don't just say fuck it and joined them is crazy to me, I don't care what they do as long as I can live at the end of the day. Those hyenas eating me alive is something I don't want to feel. I'll do whatever Black ice says not to feel that.

Then look at these tunnels. You really dug tunnels up underneath this town, that is a lot of time and work, I can't do that. I see why they're impress with your survival skills," Monica said.

"Working for Black ice is like saying yes to the devil, that he can have your soul. I just can't do that. I can't sacrifice who I am just to live, or to hurt others, it just doesn't sit right with me. I still believe in God; I still believe there is hope. I just have to escape this place again," Erica said.

"So, what you are telling me is that a crazy serial killer family kidnaps people and brings them to this place just to hunt and kill them." Monica asked.

"Pretty much. See the whole thing is that they don't exist, they leave no trace of what they do in the real world. People go missing everyday in the world, if there is no human body, law-enforcements don't make a big deal.

"Well Black ice and his children leave no bodies. They found a way to play with their victims by bringing them here. That is why there's food in here. They release people just to play with them, in some cases there is this new daughter she eats people," Erica said.

"Yeah, you are bugging they eat people, I would have screamed let me join you. I don't have time to be anyone's steak or filet mignon. I'm big as it is," Monica said.

"So, can you get us out of this place? That is the real question. You said it's hard but that means it can be done," Monica said.

Erica stopped walking and thought about what she said.

"This whole place, the woods are three to four miles long. This small town, it is all part of a bigger base, an underground compound, this isn't the first one I've been in, I think the family got them all over the world. But these bases go down three to four stories, so say we get out this area, we still have to get through the base itself, those guys you see in all black with black mask are henchmen they're trained to fight and kill, there are always twenty or more living on the base.

So, now we got to magically get past them then to see where we at, once outside.

Last time I escaped, I ended up in the middle of the real fucking woods with Black ice chasing me and my friends, so yes, the shit might can be done but I'm too tired to try it. I'd rather sit my ass where I'm at and get more information and supplies so I can be fully ready to run," Erica said as flashbacks of sleeping in the woods and jumping out her sleep every second because Black ice was close by, the hyenas laughter echoed in the night just before they attack and ate one of her friends.

"*Are you okay?*" Monica asked and touched her shoulder, snapping Erica out the trance she was in.

"*No! No, I'm not okay, I don't I'll ever be okay, neither will you after this experience. Sorry follow me we're close,*" Erica said and started walking again, then stopped at a wooden door and opened it.

"*Where are we? How the hell did you dig all of these without getting noticed?*" Monica asked as they walked in; the ceiling was taller and melted frames were all around, it was a large open space with current up in different areas for privacy.

"*I didn't, we're underneath the target building, when I started digging the tunnels, I noticed big areas under some of the homes or buildings. I decided it was the perfect way for me to hide and get a good night sleep, I go to the top to get supplies and help people. But I have the study the people I help first.*

I literally was stabbed in the back by a woman I thought was my friend and a survivor, she crossed me for Black ice," Erica said.

"So, he'll let anyone be a henchman?" Monica asked and Erica looked at her in a funny way.

I'm going to have to watch this bitch, something tells me in more than one way, she'll do anything if it means saving her life, I have been here before and will be stupid not to see the damn signs when they keep smacking me in the face. Erica thought to herself.

"No anyone can't be a henchman they add people of value to them, but that doesn't matter. What matters is you are safe now, let me introduce you to the others," Erica said.

"Others? There are other people?" Monica asked.

"It's safe to come out now," Erica said and people started coming out from behind the curtains.

"This is Luis," Erica said and pointed to a short Mexican man with a belly.

"He's very handy and helps out a lot, those two over there are Latisha and her husband Donald" Erica said trying not to show her distaste for them but rolled her eyes anyway.

"Then there is Yolanda and Kenya," Erica said.

"Shit I'm happy you are back safely, I thought Black ice has found us," Yolonda said and hugged Erica.

She was light-skinned in complexion and six feet tall with a pretty face.

"Girl, you know we got this, Black ice is not getting us without a fight." Erica replied.

"Hell yeah," Kenya said she was slim and brown-skinned in complexion with curly hair.

"So, Erica saved all of you?" Monica asked.

"Oh, I'm sorry this is Monica," Erica said introducing her to everyone.

"I thought you said there were more of them like five or six," Latisha said.

She was short and fat and dark brown in complexion, she looked good for her age fifty-five, but had a nasty attitude all the time just like her husband who didn't look as good for his age.

Donald had bald spots all over his head but you could tell he refused to let go the little hair he had and he was overweight, he looked as if he ate too much fried food, he was light-skinned in complexion, you would think he was white until he talked.

"You know how it is out there, stop acting like you don't. Everyone doesn't survive, everyone won't. It's just a fact and if people don't make it out the woods, I can't help them at all.

The woods are the only way in and out of this place and that is where the hyenas live and hunt, I can't save people unless they make it to the town and start hiding. But today was worse. Black ice and his two daughters were hunting

All of them together, it's a miracle I was able to save one person, so get off my back unless you finally going do something to contribute. You are already scared to go outside," Erica said.

"Yeah, whatever bitch, you do a horrible job at taking care of us, just give us never ending excuses and bullshit one after another on why you can't find a way out for us. Instead, we're forced to live under dirt ceiling, shitting in buckets and hear how you almost saved someone. I used to respect you, now I despise you. This isn't life, it's barely surviving," Latisha said with an attitude.

"Listen bitch you're a grown ass woman you fat hoe, you can take care of yourself. I'm tired of you always criticizing what I do. You always have something to fucking say Latisha, but you don't do shit, do you know how hard it is to go out and get some supplies, make shit happen but you talk about me having never ending stories, what do you do, how do you help.

You and your husband do not contribute to shit, all you all do is eat everything and talk about everyone.

If you can do a better job. How will you survive If I say I'm not getting more fucking food, get it yourself hoe," Erica said and stormed off.

"Hey don't talk to my wife like that, or I'll fuck you up!" Donald shouted out of breath, while shaking his fist in the air.

Erica stopped and turned around and walk up to Donald and placed a knife underneath his chin.

"I'll like to see your fat short ass try. I'll gut you like a fucking fish then drag you out while you still alive and watch the hyenas eat you, there is nothing you or your wife could do to stop me.

Put your motherfucking hands on me if you want to. Swing Donald! Fucking swing nigga. Jump you were feeling froggy a minute ago. Don't get quite now, try to take the knife out my hand. Go ahead, please!" Erica said.

Donald looked at her nervously, not knowing what to do.

"Leave my husband alone!" Latisha shouted.

"Shut the fuck up!" Erica said and smacked the living shit out of Latisha so hard, that spit and blood flew out her mouth.

"I'm tired of playing with you all. This shit not a game. Do shit for your motherfucking self," Erica said and stormed off.

Everyone else stood there watching with their eyes wide open in shock.

"You've been here too long Erica! You are starting to act like them, you even had the same crazy look in your eyes as Black ice just now bitch!" Donald shouted as the look on Erica's face played on his mind.

CHAPTER 6

Monica studied everyone, but felt comfortable with Yolanda. She sat down next to her.

"Is it always like this, we just stay down here reading books not knowing what time it is or what going on. I'm going insane," Monica said.

"You have to get used to it or there is the other option, that going out there and dying. I have seen people leave this place and never return," Yolanda replied.

"So, Erica is the only one that goes out? Monica asked. She's the only one brave enough, have you

seen what those hyenas do to a person?" Yolanda asked.

"Yeah, one of the women I was with got eaten by them. They ate her alive, like really kept her alive while ripping parts of her off," Monica replied.

"Right! They barely come in the town because of all the black pepper and Cayenne pepper Erica sprinkled everywhere, they don't like it. The taste messes with them but they still come into the stores. For some reason, the first place most people run to is the Target store. I don't know why," Yolonda said.

"That's all good but we're low on food and water and Erica just disappeared after the fight with that couple, how are we going survive. We need to get more supplies," Monica said.

"I'm not going out there, I'm not stupid. Erica usually comes back. I'll wait," Yolanda replied.

"What if she doesn't, what if she is dead somewhere, we are just going to stay down her and starve to death. If a few of us go out together

we can bring enough food back to last maybe a month.

Erica was the only person that brought things back and that kept you all fed," Monica said.

"She's right we don't need that bitch, I say we go out and get our own supplies, fuck that bitch. I'm not about to depend on anyone," Latisha said.

"Okay, then we leave now," Monica replied.

Luis stood next to Yolanda.

"I'm not going with them I know this isn't going end well," Luis said in a thick Mexican accent.

"Yeah, you are right papa, I feel safe down here and I trust Erica, she saved me and never let me down I'm not going stop trusting her cause she's upset." Yolonda replied as she watched, Monica, Latisha and her husband Donald leave.

"Where are you going?" Yolanda asked Kenya.

"Someone has to make sure they find their way back. Monica is new and we all know how smart Latisha and her husband are. They're all talk, if

we leave it up to them to actually do something they're just going fuck it up, I'll bring you back a can of those pineapple you like so much and try to get some corn beef. I got this," Kenya said then ran out after the group.

Yolanda shook her head and went back to sit down and started reading a book called parasite.

Monica tried to remember the way Erica lead her in. The tunnels were dark and long, and you could taste dust and dirt in the air. She used her flashlight to led the way, notice there were three tunnels ahead she looked back.

"Do you all remember the way out?" Monica asked.

"No! None of us goes out, only Erica does, when she saved us, we just stayed in hiding," Kenya said.

"Saved us, more like made us co-dependent on her, look at us we don't even know how to get out or can't eat without her.

My mother taught me if you give someone the power to feed you, you also give them the power to starve you. That is what she's doing, she fucking starving us, I tell you right now I'm going be no one pity party and give someone the power over my life," Latisha said.

"Not now, just let me think," Monica said.

"Okay, this way,"

Monica led them down the tunnel and found the stairs. She walked up them and looked around. They all exited the shed.

"Where should we go first for food and supplies." Kenya asked.

"There was a small store next to a restaurant. I saw it we should hit that first," Monica said.

"Who made you, boss; we should go to the Target store, it will have everything we need in one place." Latisha stated.

"Listen you can do what the fuck you like, you seem like the type of person that knows it all but

Erica told me that Target store is the first-place people go to hide if they get out the woods and the first place the hyenas and Black ice check.

That where one of women I came in here with died, so you can go," Monica said.

"Yeah, whatever bitch, like I said you don't own me," Latisha said.

"What is your problem, why do you have an attitude with everyone and everything, I don't even really know you and I don't like you," Monica said and started walking.

The town was bright with white street lights on long poles in the street.

"I have to stay on point and remember what Erica did. It's quite but I can't let that fool me," Monica said, as she looked back at Kenya.

"Listen I know you're trying to help I don't have any issues with you. Latisha always act like a bitch, she's the only one of us getting dick and she still act as if she's not getting fucked, she wants to run everything. I just want to survive another

day, knowing that this is my reality I break down and cry for no reason all the time," Kenya said.

"I know the feeling, but right now I'm too hungry to cry or feel sorry for myself and can't give two shits about Latisha's stupid ass and her husband," Monica said as they stood close to the houses like she remembered Erica doing.

She could see the corner store and ran straight to it. Kenya followed right behind her.

The corner store was filled with food and can goods and water. Monica opened a bag of hot chips and grabbed a hot pickle and opened it and started eating as if she hadn't eaten in days.

"Not for nothing, do you think that is wise, don't you think it's best we fill up on the things we need then eat once we get back," Kenya said.

Monica looked at her as if she was stupid and continued eating.

I don't think I like any one of these girls or people here. Shit, if Black ice gives me a deal, I'll tell him where they all are. Everyone is a pain in my ass and talk too fucking much especially that Latisha bitch, I'll fuck her fat ass up, she got a habit of talking to people like she's over them. I can't stand shit like that. I can see why Erica haven't return yet. She's smart probably got all kind of hideouts around this place. Don't blame her not wanting to be around people, for some reason they all piss me off. Monica thought to herself as she watched Kenya load up her black book bag with canned goods.

Latisha and Donald entered the Target store, the bright Led lights flickered off and on. Latisha nervously grabbed a shopping cart.

"Come on Donald, keep your ass close I'm going need you to protect me if anything happens," Latisha said.

"Shit, you walk too fast. You know I'm big and old and your big ass just be gliding across the floor. Just let me catch my breath," Donald replied.

"Whatever, just keep up baby," Latisha said as she started putting things in the cart as if she was in a regular grocery store.

"Oh, that's nice!" Latisha said grabbing some magazines then grabbed a few books.

"Hmmm, I don't know I'm going finish reading this one, it always has so many parts to it but I'll get it anyway," Latisha said to herself.

"Hey, baby I found the water," Donald said as he wobbled to her holding a twenty-four pack of water and put it in the cart.

"See, that fucking Erica made this seem like it was so hard to do, look we got entertainment and some canned goods, we just need a little more food and something sweet, some candy and a board game and we can get out of here. I can go back and show those bitches why I should be running shit. I don't need anyone," Latisha said as she walked down the ally and saw a baseball bat on the floor.

She picked it up to see that it had blood on it.

"I wonder what happened." She mumbled to herself as her head started to hurt.

"Where the hell is Donald, I told him to stay close," Latisha said as she heard laughter, then it stopped.

Her heart raced.

"Babe! Babe! Where are you? It's time to fucking go," Latisha said as she pushed the cart down the alley looking for her husband.

"Babe! I knew I should have married Frank; gotten with a truck driver they bring home the money and I bet he wouldn't allow us to get kidnapped.

How do you get kidnapped with a grown ass man, I blame myself, fell in love with a man all because of the way he ate my ass, now look at me overweight with a fat man that wobbles when he walks, and kidnapped.

Let me stop bitches, I wonder if I do a lot that is why I don't have any friends. Nah, I'm not the problem people are," Latisha said to herself while looking for her husband.

The Led lights started to flicker even more, leaving it darker for a longer time now. Latisha grabbed the baseball bat. She looked down an alley and squinted her eyes as the light flicked out.

Her eyes opened wide as she saw the silhouette of a man standing there with a machete in his hand. She screamed and the lights flickered back on and no one was there.

"Oh, fuck no! Nope! I don't do the horror scary shit. I never did and am not about to start now. Donald I'm about to leave your ass. I read one or two scary books to know this the part the black person runs. I'm seeing shit. That can't be good for my health," Latisha said then started pushing her cart down the ally, making her way to the front of the store.

The light flickered out again and she could see six pairs of red eyes blinking and staring at her and the silhouette of a man in a trench coat standing in between them, with a cigarette in his mouth. He pulled on it and the flame in it glowed bright.

The light flickered on and no one was there.

"Nope fuck this food! I'm out," Latisha said and left the cart and started walking back away from the front door.

"Donald babe! Please help! Where are you? I think Black ice is here and I'm fucking two second away from pissing on myself. You supposed to be my big strong husband," Latisha whispered while walking fast down another ally trying to make her way to the back of the store.

"I knew I should have married Frank," Latisha mumbled then screamed as she heard footsteps running toward her fast, just as the light flickered out.

As soon as it got close Latisha swung with all her might, just as the light flicked back on. The bat slam Donald in the side of the head he dropped to the floor onto his ass while holding his stomach.

"Stupid I could have killed you. You don't run up on any black person when the light is off, now get

up, I got a bad feeling. I think Black ice is here," Latisha said talking and looking around as if someone was going jump out if nowhere and try to rob her.

The light flickered brighter and she looked down and really noticed Donald for the first time. His right eye ball was hanging out the socket by a thin piece of skin, just bouncing up and down. He looked as if he was crying and trying to talk.

His left hand was on his stomach on his fat stomach covered in blood along with his shirt soaking in it. He raised his right arm.

"Ahhh!" Latisha let out a faint scream and covered her mouth then looked around and back at his arm to see his hand was chopped off.

"Baby what happened? Stand up, let me get you out of here!" Latisha said as she grabbed his left arm and tried to lift him up, then heard something skipping on the floor making a thumping sound, it slid to her feet.

Her eyes opened up wide to see that it was Donald's detached Hand.

"I thought I'll give you a helping hand," Black ice said and smirked then lit his cigarette full of crack as he watched them from a few feet away with a hyena by his side.

"Come on get up baby! Get up now!" Latisha shouted as Black ice walked slowly toward them smiling.

"Baby please get the fuck up now!" Latisha said as she started to cry.

Donald was finally able to stand up but stumbled a little. He held onto his stomach tightly as Latisha pulled his arm.

"Wait don't pull my arm," he said weakly, barely able to speak because of the agonizing pain he was in.

"Shut up! I need you to stay alive, to do that you must run! I need you to run fool, as much you get in my nerves and piss me off, I can't live without you. You're my husband, I need you!" Latisha

shouted louder as they turned and cut through an ally and could see the door to the back storage for the store.

Latisha yanked Donald arm even harder then, Donald stopped running and stood still.

"I told you not to pull my arm," Donald said as blood poured out his stomach.

Latisha looked down at his stomach to see a long slash through his shirt on his big belly.

"Ahh!" Latisha hollered as his intestines started to fell out on the ground.

Donald dropped to his knees. Latisha looked on in horror then stumbled forward when something hit her in the back of the head, she fell face first into Donald's guts, she spat as parts of him entered her mouth and Donald fell, sideways groaning in pain.

"Ughh! I told you to run baby! Get it up and run!" Donald said weakly as he tried to keep his stomach from keep falling out. He laid on the ground on his side breathing shallow.

Latisha tried to get up but couldn't. She could feel big hands on her back, she turned around to see Black ice pushing and pinning her down with his pants down and dick hard in his left hand.

"No! No!" Latisha shouted and tried to squirm and get away but he was too strong.

"Stay the fuck still, you're like a big old pig, just squirming around," He said as he spat on his hand and wiped it on the tip of his duck and ripped off Latisha's Spandex.

"Ahh!" Latisha screamed as the tip of his dick worked its way into her anal, with each stroke he pushed it in more inch by inch.

"No! No stop! Get off me! Stop! Donald help." Latisha screamed but Donald just laid there looking at her barely able to moving while breathing shallow.

Latisha eyes opened up wider as she felt all of Black ice dick inside her.

"Oh God! Oh God!" She moaned as it started to feel good.

Why am I getting wet? And why is it starting to feel good. His dick is scratching me the hell out. Latisha thought to herself while moaning.

"Oh God! Yes! Yes," she screamed as Black ice pumped his thick long chocolate dick in and out of her, he grinded his hips as he pushed his dick all the way inside her, then slapped Latisha hard on the face.

"You like that piggy! Say you fucking love it piggy!" Black ice said then slapped her on the forehead.

"Say you love it piggy!" He said in a deep tone voice and started stroking even harder and faster.

"I love it! I love it," Latisha screamed while crying because she really was enjoying it, his penis was hitting spots she didn't know about.

She opened her eyes to see her husband Donald looking at her as he bled out slowly. The look of despair and hurt was written in his face.

"Baby I'm sorry!" Latisha said then got slap in the face again.

"Shut the fuck up piggy, let him watch you get fucked by a real nigga piggy!" Black ice said then slapped her twice.

"I want you to fucking squeal like a pig bitch!" Black ice shouted.

"Huh! What?" Latisha said and tried to get up but he pushed her back down. Black ice punched her in the rib.

Latisha screamed and gasped for air, as she tried to catch her breath but couldn't because he didn't stop stroking inside her.

"I said squeal like pig bitch!" Black ice said and slap her on the forehead.

Latisha started to squeal like a pig.

"Oink! Oink! Oink!"

"Yeah, just like that piggy! Squeal while I ride that ass bitch! I can't hear you! Louder! Louder!" Black ice shouted and slap her on the forehead repeatedly then the face.

"Oink! Oink!" Latisha said and could feel his thick throbbing inside her then exploded as he came shooting cum all up in her ass.

Black ice wiped the tip of his penis on her shirt, then stood up.

"That was good piggy, you are a good little piggy," Black ice said in a deep tone as he pulled up his pants than pulled out his machete.

"It's over, he's going kill me now, God save me." Latisha cried out loud then looked at Donald who was staring at her crying hysterically, then she could see Black ice stand over him and smirk as his eyes made contact with her.

"Are you watching piggy! I want you to pay attention," Black ice said then swung.

"Ahh! Ahh!" Donald hollered at the top of his lungs as Black ice chopped off his leg from his

thigh up and tossed it behind him to two hyenas.

"Ah! Latisha! Latisha! Ahh! It's hurts! It hurts!" Donald screamed while crying, his voice whimpering.

"Ahh!" He started screaming again as Black started to chop of his next leg.

"Damn you are a big guy, it took two swings for me to chop that off. Do you know how crazy that sounds because my strength is beyond normal," Black ice said as he picked up Donald's detached leg and threw it to the hyenas behind him, then he placed his machete blade on Donald's neck.

"Are you watching piggy, I got to line this up just right. He is fat, he really doesn't have a neck. If I miss it will be very messy bitch. Keep watching piggy," Black ice said in a dark tone.

"No! Please don't!" Latisha screamed.

Donald was in shock and his body was shaking as he laid on his side. White foam was coming out of his mouth.

Black ice looked at Latisha and smiled then swung, chopping Donald's head clean off, it rolled over and stopped right in front of Latisha.

"Ahh! Ahh! Donald! Donald!" Latisha screamed while crying hysterically and jumped up and started running.

She looked back to see Black ice kicking Donald's head around like a soccer ball, then he looked up at her and waved while smiling.

Latisha turned around with Black ice smile stuck in her head as she ran faster and could see the back exit to the store but next to it was a table with a white cloth in it with candles lit up and rose petals on the floor.

No, I shouldn't go that way. Something isn't right. Why the hell is a romantic setup by the door. Why would a table be there, but I can't go back, Black ice is there; Fuck I'll take my chance. Latisha thought to herself and ran past to the table and made it to the steel exist door. She grabbed the door knob and didn't see the black snake until it was too late.

It bit her on the hand.

"Ouch!" Latisha said and backpedaled while rubbing her hand and looked at the snake on the door.

"Why do I feel dizzy? Was the snake poisonous? Is black snake poisonous," Latisha asked herself and dropped the ground and couldn't move.

Black ice walked over to her holding Donald's head.

"Kiss him one last time," Black ice said sarcastically and press Donald's lips against hers.

"Please! Please don't hurt me!" Latisha said as she tried to move but couldn't.

"I'm done with you piggy. I've had my fun, you belong to my middle child now, well I think she's

my middle child I can't tell anymore, I got too many kids but she's one of my favorite. The problem is, feeding the little bitch. She's always hungry and eats like a grown damn man, shit I'd rather clothe her than feed her but it is what it is. Bye piggy," Black ice said in a dark demonic tone as he walked off, throwing Donald's head in the air and catching it as if it was a basketball.

Latisha sat on the floor crying while trying to move but couldn't she could hear footsteps than felt someone's hands lift her up.

He's back, who else is strong enough to lift me up. Latisha thought to herself knowing she was short and fat and weighed 270 pounds.

Someone sat her in a chair at the table.

Latisha looked around the table, there was a hotpot for portable cooking on it and candles, a bottle of red wine and a fancy plate.

A young woman walked around the table no older than twenty.

"Hi piggy, I'm Yana nice to meet you," Yana said.

"Why can't I move?" Latisha asked.

"That is because of mamas," Yana replied.

"What is a mamas?" Latisha asked as she tried to move but could only talk, then a snake slithered across the floor and slithered up Yana's leg, onto her shoulder then sat there.

"You've met mamas, her venom can paralyze her victims or can kill them depending on the situation but she has gotten much better at using it. One time she used too little and let's just say that was a mess," Yana said as she stir some white rice on the hot plate then brought out another pot.

She looks harmless, maybe if I keep talking to her. I can get her to like me. I can talk myself out this situation somehow. Latisha thought to herself.

"You seem nice," Latisha said, then for the first time she had seen it, when Yana smiled. It was the same devilish evil smirk Black ice had.

Yana smiled then laughed.

"Only if my sisters could hear you say that. I'm the mean one, not nice at all. Normally, I don't talk so much but going through some issues with my triplet sisters, one has gone crazy and one is just evil as fuck and was never really talking then, there is Osis, my surrogate sister who I miss the most, the only person I really had to talk to, until one of my sisters murdered her.

So, now I talk to my food before I eat," Yana said.

Latisha studied her. Yana was dark-skinned in complexion a beautiful chocolate, with white teeth and a curly hair wig on with baby hairs on it. She was kind of tall look to be 5'8 and the way she talked you could tell she was from the hood.

"Please, just let me go!" Latisha said and tried to move again but couldn't.

"Now why would I do that piggy," Yana said sounding just like her father.

"See, I lived on a Caribbean Island for a few years, while I was there, I fell in love with the food, it

was amazing. But one dish stuck out to me, that I had to learn how to make," Yana said.

Well play along until I can talk the stupid young girl to let me go. Latisha thought to herself.

"What was the dish?" Latisha asked not really caring.

"Curry, I fucking love curry anything at this point. It's the best thing I tasted and I got really good at cooking it, had to watch so many YouTube videos you just don't understand," Yana said and pulled out a small portable grinder saw.

Latisha's heart raced.

"What are you going do with that?" Latisha asked.

"I have another craving something I could never understand since I was a teenager but you know some cultures eat goat head and goat brains, I felt normal after learning that.

Even went to one of the restaurants for the goat head. It was delicious but not as good as I cook." Yana replied.

"Uhm, you still didn't answer me. What are you going do with that small power saw in your hand?" Latisha asked not really wanting to know the answer.

"Oh, my bad, I'm going cut open only the top part of your skull and I'm good at doing it, so I can keep you alive, then I'm going take a nice chunk of your brain and put it into the curry I started cooking then I'm going sit down with a glass of red wine and eat your curry brain with potatoes and carrots and white rice and smile with each bite," Yana said as she walked to Latisha.

"No please! Don't you touch me! No, you little bitch!" Latisha screamed then started crying as the saw came on and she could feel it cutting through her flesh.

"Ahh! Ahh!" She screamed as the pain was more than she could bear.

Blood from her forehead drip down into her eyes.

"Ah! God! God save me!" Latisha screamed then the saw stopped.

Latisha prayed it was over.

"God is not going to save you. All of you pray for that at this moment," Yana said then smiled her devilish grin then started pulling until she pulled off the top skull off of Latisha's head.

"Ahh!" Latisha let out a piercing scream while crying out in agonizing pain.

Her last words as Yana grabbed half her brain and ripped it out was; *"I should have married Frank."*

CHAPTER 7

"Did you hear that? It sounded like Latisha," Kenya said as she finished stuffing her bag with goods then grabbed two gallons of water and put them in plastic bag.

"Yeah, that was a loud scream, maybe she's yelling at her husband again," Monica said.

"I doubt that, one thing Erica said is that we should stay away from the target store." Kenya replied.

"Naw, they'll be fine, let's grab some more stuff then go hide in one of these houses, there is no point in staying underneath the ground. It's hot

down there and dusty as hell. I'm starting to think we can live up here," Monica said.

Kenya looked at her as if she was stupid or dumb.

"Have you lost your mind?" Kenya asked.

"Why did you say that?" Monica asked.

"Because I think you have forgetting where you at. This isn't a real store, those houses yes, are real on the outside and inside but this isn't a real place, think of it like a movie set, it looks real and feels real but we're still in hell in the devil's playground where he hunts and his children play. This isn't some place you relax, just because you feel comfortable or nothing bad has happened in a while.

That loud as scream we just heard most likely means, Latisha smart ass mouth is dead or dying or being killed. Don't forget where you are. This isn't a dream or nightmare and we're not really outside," Kenya said looking at Monica as if she was crazy.

"Yeah, I heard you but I think we can make our own rules or even a deal with Black ice, I'd rather stay in one of these homes than hide underground. I don't think it's as bad as Erica said it is," Monica replied.

"You've been with us a few days and already forgot what you been through to get to this point. Shit is mind blowing how slow people are, I'm out of here." Kenya replied and as she put the book bag in her back and grabbed her bags that held the water and walked out the store.

"Stupid bitch but I'm not trying to be left alone," Monica said and grabbed her book bag and left the store then stopped when she heard groaning and someone asking for help.

"You hear that?" Monica said.

Kenya was ahead of her and looked back.

"Yeah, I do but that shit doesn't concern us. We got what we needed. Let's just keep moving," Kenya said.

"It's coming from that restaurant, I'm going help," Monica said and walked toward the restaurant.

Kenya looked back and suck3d her teeth.

"Fuck! If I leave her, I'll be wrong right. That's what would happen. But she's not listening, she does too much. Fuck," Kenya said and put her bags down by a house then went after Monica.

Monica reached the hibachi style restaurant. She pushed open the door and could hear groaning.

Monica pulled out the kitchen knife. There were a few lights on. Kenya came in behind her.

"We shouldn't be here. We need to leave I got a bad feeling." Kenya said.

"Shh! Quite did you hear that," Monica said.

"Help me! Help me please!" A voice said but the words sound disorientated as if a baby was talking and couldn't speak properly.

"It's coming from the kitchen," Monica said and walked to the back of the restaurant and pushed the kitchen door open.

The kitchen was bright from the Led lights and steel countertops and table.

 Monica could see Stephanie standing there naked holding the steel countertop. Her back was covered in bite marks with blood dripping out of them, more bite marks were on her butt cheeks. Blood was dripping from between her legs down her thigh.

"Oh my God, what did they do to you?" Monica said and rush over to her and grab her by the shoulder to turn her around.

When she did, Monica and Kenya both screamed.

"Ahh!"

The sight of Stephanie was the most disgusting and horrifying thing they had ever seen. Her eyes were dug out, all you could see was bloody black eye sockets. Her ears had been cut off and her tongue cut out of her mouth. She felt around to try and touch Monica.

"Help me! Please help me before he comes back! Help me," Stephanie said as she tried to touch Monica.

Her words sounded discombobulated.

"Before who comes back?" Monica said then heard footsteps as if someone was walking to her in high heel.

 Stephanie started to whimper as if she was trying not to cry.

"He's back! He's back!" Stephanie said as her body started to tremble and she urinated on herself.

Monica stepped back as she saw Brock walking towards them. He was taller than the tables and countertops. He stood next to Stephanie. Stephanie cried and sat down on the floor.

Brock looked at Kenya and Monica.

 "I think we should run," Kenya said.

"You know what? For once I think your right," Monica said and they took off running.

Brock tilted his head high up and hollered.

Monica and Kenya rushed out of the stores to only see hyenas running down the hill from the woods.

"Shit, I think he called his friends on us," Monica said as the hyenas started chasing them.

Kenya was lighter and faster.

"You think so! I told you not to go in there. I warn your stupid ass now look," Kenya said as she ran behind a house then ran down a block.

Monica struggled to keep up. She was overweight and didn't walk at all in everyday life unless she had to. She looked back to see that the hyenas were still coming, laughing as they ran.

"I thought Erica said they don't come down here," Monica said while getting tired.

"No, she said they don't like the smell of the pepper while looking for us. They don't have to look for us. They see us right now," Kenya said sarcastically as they duck behind a house.

"I can't keep up. You're too fast," Monica said as she hid with Kenya.

Kenya looked down the block to see more hyenas.

"We are going have to hop that fence and keep running until we make it to the shed. Just try to keep up," Kenya said.

"You know that's a good idea," Monica said then stabbed Kenya in the back of her left thigh.

"Ahh!" Kenya screamed and turned around and punched her.

Monica stabbed her again this time on the back and took off run.

"You bitch! You fucking bitch," Kenya said as she tried to run but couldn't.

Her loud scream from a second ago had attracted the hyenas.

One jumped on her back knocking her to the ground. The hyenas wasted no time to rip Kenya's arms and legs off and started eating them.

"Ahh!" Kenya screamed as she watched Monica climb the fence and run toward the shed, then entered it and the secret tunnel.

She could hear Kenya scream while still being eaten alive. Monica ran through the tunnels as fast as she could.

 "It was her or me, and it damn sure wasn't going be me," Monica said and smiled as she made it to the hideout door, she opened it and her heart sunk in her chest.

Yolanda and Luis were ripped to shred, their body parts all over the hide out and six hyenas was eating them.

Monica backpedaled without making a sound. She turned around to and flinched when she saw Erica.

"Oh shit! It's just you. Where have you been?" Monica said then notice Erica had fresh clothing on.

She was dressed in all black.

"I took your advice and said yes. There is no point in me living underground or hiding, no point in waiting for someone like you to stab me in the back like you just did Kenya," Erica said.

"I did what I had to and I'll do it again. I'll stab you so those hyenas will eat you before they get to me," Monica said as she pulled out a knife, ready to stab Erica.

Erica pulled out a hand gun and pointed at Monica head.

"Yeah, I made the right decision." Erica said as she pulled out a black henchmen mask and put it on then shot Monica on the knee cap.

"Thank you for helping make the choice," Erica said as she turned around and six hyenas were behind her. She walked right past them as they stared at Monica and started to laugh.

"No! No, don't leave me! No!" Monica screamed as the hyenas rushed her.

CHAPTER 8

Michael stood at the roof looking at the warehouse.

"I know you're there I can feel your energy," Michael said to himself while crying.

"I'll kill you I swear I'll kill you," he said as he wiped his tears.

"You always were soft and had too much of your mother in you. I don't need you anymore now I have my daughters."

Michael heard his father voice whisper in his ear.

Michael tried to turn around and pulled out his machete but was too slow as Black ice swung and chopped off his head.

His head went flying in the air and Black ice front kick his body, it fell off the roof. Black ice picked up Michael head then started bouncing it off his knees like a soccer ball.

"Like I said weak like your mother," Black ice said as he held his son head like a football under his arm and lit a cigarette filled with crack.

"Michael!" Rachel shouted jumping out her sleep covered in sweat.

"Another dream, God please keep my baby safe. He's still my son no matter if he has his father blood in him," Rachel said then grabbed her shotgun and cellphone.

"Maybe he'll listen to me. That's the third time I had that dream. He must listen to me," Rachel said to herself as she called him but as his phone rang, she could hear ringing in her house.

Rachel gripped her shotgun and walked out her bedroom ready for anything. She followed the ringing to her living and turned on the light to see a blue present box on her coffee table. She walked to it and opened it, to see Michael's phone then post card.

Rachel picked up the post card and read it.

"Congratulations you're no longer my baby mother. Huh what the hell," Rachel said then looked inside the box and could see Michael's detached head, his eyes looking at her.

"No! Not my baby! Lord not my baby! Why did you let the devil take him, No!" Rachel cried hysterically as she dropped to her knees.

Black ice stood across the street from her house smoking a cigarette filled with crack with his evil smile on his face as he listened to her screams.

A CHILD OF A CRACK HEAD 7.

~RACHEAL'S REVENGE~

Paula and Ella unloaded the groceries.

"This cookout is going be just what I need," Paula said as black amazon van pulled up to their driveway.

"You are expecting a delivery?" Paula asked.

"Yeah, I ordered a few things on Amazon." Ella replied but didn't see the two men that got out the black amazon van until it was too late.

One tapped her on the shoulder. She turned around to see a man dress in all black with a black mask. He sprayed her in the face with something and she lost consciousness.

Ella walked out the house and noticed Paula was gone. She went to the trunk of the car to see they still had more groceries to unload. She felt a tap on her shoulder then got sprayed in the face.

Before she could hit the ground, she could feel her body being lifted up and carried to the back of the van.

"You can let her go right now!" Rachel said.

The two henchmen turned around to see her pointing a gun at them. They laughed.

"Our mask and suit is bulletproof bitch," One of the henchmen said and Rachel squeezed the trigger and the shotgun roar.

The shotgun pellets slammed into the henchmen face mask and his head exploded like a melon hit with a sledgehammer.

"Oh shit!" The second henchmen said, then turn back and look at Rachel.

"You know who I am?" Rachel asked.

"Yeah, you're his baby mother, the first one," The henchmen said nervously.

"Wrong I'm the one God sent to end him. Where is he? Where is Black ice!" Rachel said through clenched teeth.

"I don't know, he doesn't tell us his movement and even if I did. I'm more scared of him than you," the henchman said then tried to reach for his gun.

Rachel squeezed the trigger the shotgun roar again blowing a huge hole into the chest and back of the henchman.

He flew backward and slid down the van, but was still was alive, groaning in pain.

"Don't worry I'll find him on my own but you should fear me more. God is on my side!" Rachel said and squeezed the trigger once more and the henchman's face exploded.

Rachel opened the back of the van doors, to see four women tied up.

She threw a knife to one.

"Thank you! Thank you," the woman said as she cut the rope.

"Who are you?" Another one asked.

"The one that going kill all these bastards, Until I kill the man that hurt me all my life," Rachel said then walked away.

Made in the USA
Monee, IL
19 May 2025

17777473R00075